# Who's on First?

BY

## ABBOTT & COSTELLO

ILLUSTRATED BY JOHN MARTZ

QUIRK BOOKS

PHILADELPHIA

Hiya
Abbott!

Say, if you're the coach, you must know all the players, right?

I sure do!

Well, I've never met the guys. Will you tell me their names?

Certainly! But I'll warn you — baseball players do have some funny names these days.

Now let's see...

**WHO's** on first.

**WHAT's** on second.

**I DON'T KNOW's** on third.

WHO'S on second?

Who is on FIRST!

I DON'T KNOW!

THIRD BASE!

# THIRD BASE!

The left fielder's name?

WHY!

Because!

Oh, he's center field.

BECAUSE

Okay. What time?

What time what?

What time tomorrow are you gonna tell me who's pitching?

Now listen:

**WHO** is not pitching!

So, I get behind the plate to do some fancy catching.

Tomorrow's pitching on my team...

...and a heavy hitter gets up.

Now the heavy hitter bunts the ball.

When he bunts the ball, me, being a good catcher, I'm gonna throw the guy out at first.

So I pick up the ball and I throw it to **WHO?**

Now that's the first thing you've said right!

I DON'T EVEN KNOW WHAT I'M TALKING ABOUT!

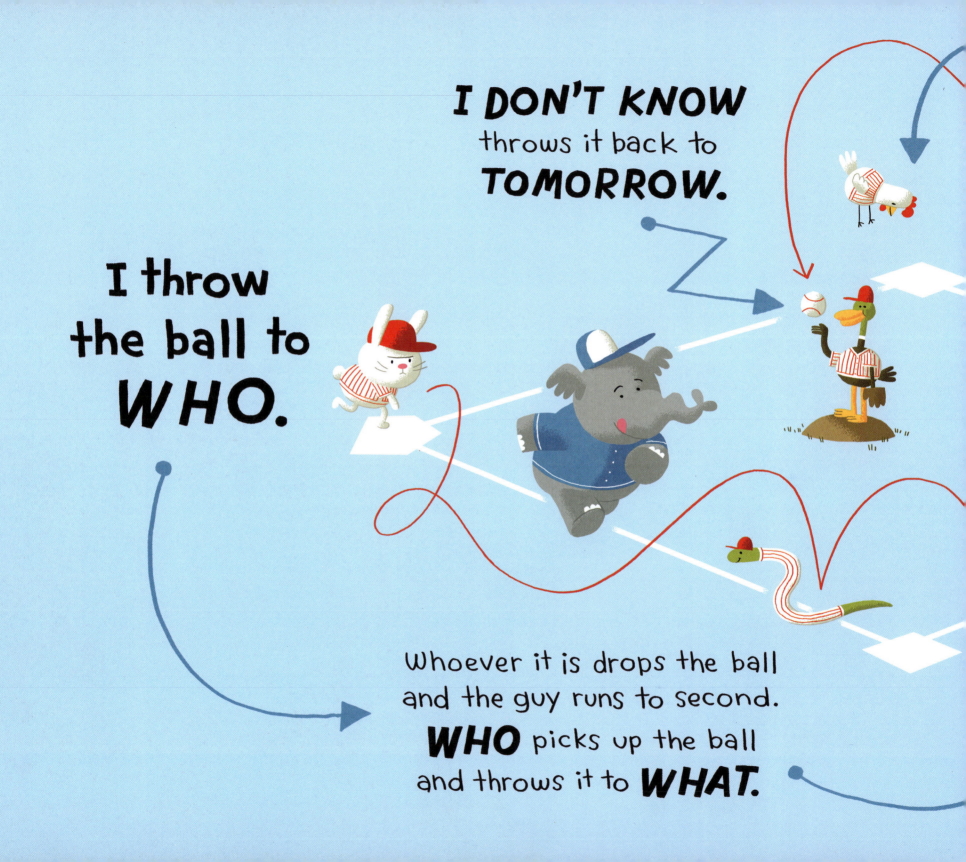

Another guy gets up and hits a long flyball to **BECAUSE.**

**WHY?** **I DON'T KNOW!**

He's on **THIRD** and... **I... DON'T... GIVE A HOOT!**

Oh that's our shortstop.

# A Brief History of "Who's on First?"

"Who's on First?" is one of the most famous comedy skits of all time. It was introduced by comedians Bud Abbott and Lou Costello in the 1930s, and they performed it many times over the course of their careers (often with subtle changes and variations). You can see a short version of their performance in the 1940 film *One Night in the Tropics* and a longer version in the 1945 film *The Naughty Nineties*.

Today, Abbott and Costello are among the few nonathletes represented in the National Baseball Hall of Fame and Museum in Cooperstown, New York. In 1956, a gold record of "Who's on First?" was placed in the museum, and a video of the routine (from *The Naughty Nineties*) plays continuously for visitors to enjoy. In 1999, *Time* magazine named "Who's on First?" the best comedy sketch of the 20th century.

Library of Congress Cataloging in Publication Number:
2012934522

ISBN: 978-1-59474-590-4

Printed in China

Designed by Doogie Horner
Production management by John J. McGurk

Quirk Books
215 Church Street
Philadelphia, PA 19106
quirkbooks.com

10 9 8 7 6 5 4 3 2 1